What she saw made the blood drain from her face in terror. . . .

An eye, a huge, blue human eye, was against the window, looking in at her. It blinked.

Trembling, Susan backed against the door. She tried to scream, but nothing came out. She couldn't make a sound.

She tried again. Still nothing.

The enormous, staring eye backed away, and she saw a huge head with big tufts of white hair outside the window.

It was Jeremy Tidwell, the owner of the toy shop! He was smiling, as if he could see her—as if he were pleased with what he saw.

I'm a doll, and this is a dollhouse, Susan thought frantically. *My wishes really* have *come true. I'm living in the dollhouse. And I'm trapped in here forever!*

Find out where the evil will strike next at

DOOMSDAY
MALL

Look for these books:

#2 The Hunt

#3 The Beast

#4 The Witch

DOOMSDAY MALL

The Dollhouse

Bebe Faas Rice

BANTAM BOOKS
NEW YORK · TORONTO · LONDON · SYDNEY · AUCKLAND

RL 4, 008-012

THE DOLLHOUSE
A Bantam Book / September 1995

Produced by Daniel Weiss Associates, Inc.
33 West 17th Street
New York, NY 10011

Cover art by Jim Thiesen

ISBN: 0-553-48180-0

Published simultaneously in the United States and Canada

Bantam Books are published by Bantam Books, a division of Bantam
Doubleday Dell Publishing Group, Inc. Its trademark, consisting of the
words "Bantam Books" and the portrayal of a rooster, is Registered in the
U.S. Patent and Trademark Office and in other countries. Marca
Registrada. Bantam Books, 1540 Broadway, New York, New York 10036.

PRINTED IN THE UNITED STATES OF AMERICA

OPM   0 9 8 7 6 5 4 3 2 1

To David Ford Rice—
Welcome to the world.

WELCOME TO
DOOMSDAY MALL . . .

. . . where kids love to hang out, where stores are always packed, where fun is guaranteed.

And where evil awaits.

Evil you can't see until it's too late.

Evil that lies buried with the deadly secret of Doomsday Mall.

And until the secret is revealed, the horror will never end.

Upper Level

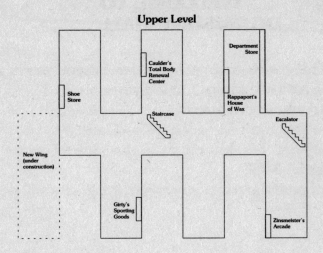

Shoe Store

Caulder's Total Body Renewal Center

Staircase

Department Store

Rappaport's House of Wax

Escalator

New Wing (under construction)

Girty's Sporting Goods

Zinsmeister's Arcade

You Are Here

Lower Level

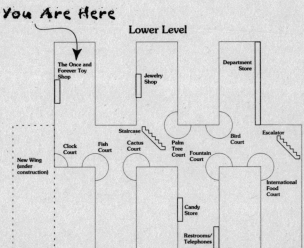

The Once and Forever Toy Shop

Jewelry Shop

Department Store

Staircase

Clock Court

Fish Court

Cactus Court

Palm Tree Court

Fountain Court

Bird Court

Escalator

New Wing (under construction)

Candy Store

Restrooms/ Telephones

International Food Court

Prologue

There was something evil about the hill.

Even the early Indian tribes wouldn't go near it.

It was haunted, their legends told them. Nothing grew there. No animals or birds were ever seen on the large rise of land that stood like a diseased growth on the landscape.

Maybe that's why the first colonists who'd settled nearby built their gallows there and called it Hangman's Hill, and buried the executed criminals beside the gallows, in rocky, unmarked graves.

Many criminals had been hanged there. Murderers. Thieves. Kidnappers. But today was special. Today was the day they were executing a sorcerer—a man who practiced enchantments and black magic.

The town elders, grim-faced under their powdered white wigs, accompanied the sorcerer to the gallows where the hangman waited.

The sorcerer didn't look wicked—or even dangerous. He looked old. Old and frail, with wispy white hair and pale, watery blue eyes.

He'd come to town one day out of nowhere, driving a gaily painted peddler's wagon. And in that shiny, colorful wagon was something very special for each and every one of his customers. It wasn't until . . . afterward . . . that they found to their horror that the real price for their hearts' desires was more, much more, than they'd bargained for.

The hangman settled the heavy noose around the neck of the sorcerer.

The sorcerer smiled.

What happened next was something that would be debated and discussed in the village for many years to come.

Some people claimed the sorcerer disappeared in a puff of smoke. Others said that when he turned those pale-blue eyes on them, they went into a deep, hypnotic trance and were unable to remember later just what, exactly, had happened.

Others said that this was all foolishness—that the sorcerer died on the gallows jut like any other criminal and was buried in a deep, deep grave on Hangman's Hill . . .

One

MALL—NEXT EXIT, the sign said. FINE STORES AND SPE-
CIALTY SHOPS! INTERNATIONAL FOOD COURT!

Food court? That meant pizzas. Cheeseburgers.
Tacos.

Bingo!

"I'm hungry," Susan said.

She leaned forward, her chin resting on the
back of the front seat, and said it again, just in case
her parents hadn't heard her the first time. "I'm
hungry. Starving to death hungry."

Mrs. Martin looked at her watch.

"Well, it *is* lunchtime, Henry," she told Susan's
father. "And there won't be any food in the new
house."

"The fridge probably won't even be plugged in,"
Susan added.

"I hate malls," Mr. Martin said tiredly. "All those

people. Can't we find a nice, quiet restaurant?"

Mrs. Martin pulled a shopping list from her purse and glanced at it. "Actually, this will save me a trip later. We'll need a new shower curtain, among other things, if we're all going to clean up tonight."

Mr. Martin sighed and pulled over to the exit lane. "Well, all right."

Susan reached into the space-age kiddie seat beside her and gently nudged her baby brother's chubby little arm.

"Did you hear that, Howie? Lunch at the mall. That means pizza, big guy."

Howie's round blue eyes lit up. "Piz-za!"

Howie was just learning to talk. So far he knew three words: Ma-ma, Da-da, and piz-za.

"Piz-za! Piz-za!" Howie chanted happily as Mr. Martin drove down the exit ramp and headed the car in the direction of the mall.

Susan brushed her long brown hair out of her eyes and stared out the window. The mall looked brand new, even at a distance. Its whitewashed brick and concrete glittered in the sun.

And it was big. Huge, in fact. It sprawled across the top of what must have once been a large hill. Mr. Martin pulled into the vast outdoor parking area and found a spot near a little brick walkway that led to one of the entrances. Over it was a striped awning with the sign:

INTERNATIONAL FOOD COURT
FOOD FROM AROUND THE WORLD

Susan grinned. "Let's eat!"

As they walked through the wide, heavy glass doors into the coolness of the mall, a funny little shiver went down Susan's spine.

"It's cold in here," she said, shivering again.

"It feels just right to me," said her mother.

Mr. Martin shifted Howie to his other shoulder. "Your Irish great-grandmother would have said that a goose just walked over your grave, Susan."

"What does that mean?" Susan asked worriedly.

"Nothing," replied her father. "It's just an old saying."

"Really, Henry," Mrs. Martin said with a frown. "You don't need to upset the children with Granny's spooky old sayings."

"Piz-za! Piz-za!" shouted Howie.

Mr. Martin chuckled. "Howie doesn't sound upset."

Susan's mother settled herself and Howie at a table in the court while Susan and her father went to the take-out counters for their orders.

Susan's father went to the All-American Salad Bar for his wife and the Roast Beef of Olde England sandwich counter for himself.

Susan went to Viva Vinnie's for her taco and the Tower of Pasta for Howie's pizza.

"Easy on the sauce," she told the man behind the counter. "It's for my baby brother."

The man raised his eyebrows.

"He eats only the cheese," Susan explained. "And he likes to gum the crust. He's getting some new teeth."

When Susan brought the food to the table, she found Howie being admired by a couple of elderly ladies at the next table.

Susan rolled her eyes. Howie had that effect on people. Particularly older women.

His pale-yellow hair was the same color and texture as a baby chick's fuzz, and it stood up on his head the same way, too. No amount of brushing would make it stay down.

"Piz-za! Piz-za!" exclaimed Howie, thumping the table.

Soon everyone was busily gulping down their food.

Susan glanced around the food court. "This mall is bigger than the one back home," she said thoughtfully.

Her mother smiled. "Then maybe this move

won't be quite as terrible as you thought. You know how much you love going to malls."

"But not by myself." Susan put down her taco. Her appetite had suddenly vanished. "I always went with Donna. I miss her already."

Mrs. Martin reached over and laid her hand on Susan's. "You'll make new friends, sweetie. Believe me."

"That's easy for you to say, Mom. You don't have to worry about starting a new school. By sixth grade, everyone's had best friends for years and years!" Susan sighed deeply. "That's how it was with Donna and me, anyway."

Susan's parents exchanged anxious glances across the table.

"Look, Susie," said her father. "You know we had no choice. We had to come here because of my job."

"Yeah, but—"

"That's the way it is, and you might as well get used to it," he said. "Anyway, once we're settled in our new neighborhood, I know you're going to meet some nice kids."

"Maybe." Susan wasn't sure. Parents *always* said stuff like that.

"Besides," added her mom, "I just know you're going to love our new house."

The thought of her new house took Susan's mind off Donna for a moment. Dad and Mom kept saying how beautiful it was, but they refused to describe it.

"Why won't you tell me anything about the new house?" she asked, biting into her taco again.

"Because I want it to be a surprise," her dad said with a sly grin. "I want to see the look on your face when we get there."

"It's really that nice?"

"I think so. Don't you, Marion?"

"I still don't know how you got it at that price, Henry," Mrs. Martin said. "What a good deal! You certainly have a nose for real estate."

Susan's father looked very pleased with himself.

Mrs. Martin glanced hurriedly at her watch. "And speaking of the new house, I'd better get my shopping done. The movers are supposed to arrive with the furniture sometime this afternoon."

"Where are you going?" Susan asked.

"There's bound to be a bed and bath shop around here somewhere," her mother said, looking around. "I need things for the main bathroom."

"Could I go off on my own, then, while you're shopping?" Susan asked. "Donna's birthday is coming up. I'd like to start looking for the perfect present."

Her mother wrinkled her nose. "I don't know, Susan. This is a new mall. You don't know your way around. You'll get lost."

"No I won't, Mom. There are always big maps everywhere in malls. You know, with a big X to show you exactly where you are."

Mrs. Martin looked doubtful.

"Look, Mom, how long are you going to be? A half hour? I'll meet you right here in a half hour, okay?"

"We-ell," said her mother.

"I think Susan will be all right on her own for a half hour, Marion," Mr. Martin said evenly, wiping cheese off Howie's chin.

"Thanks, Dad." Susan shot him a grateful grin.

"A half hour now, remember?" repeated her mother.

"Are you wearing your watch?" asked her father.

She held up her arm with the Mickey Mouse watch. Then she saluted her father. "A half an hour, sir. On the dot!"

She clicked her heels together, no easy job in a pair of sneakers, and marched briskly away.

Her father laughed.

"If you think she's bad now, wait until she's a teenager," she heard her mother say.

*   *   *

9

Susan walked slowly through the main hall, trying to figure out what to get Donna for her birthday next month. It had to be something special. She wanted Donna to know that she missed her and that she wouldn't forget her.

She stopped and peered into the window of a costume jewelry shop. She and Donna were dying to have their ears pierced, but both of their mothers said they had to wait until next year. Really! She and Donna were nearly twelve. All the other girls their age were wearing earrings already.

Susan sighed and moved on. Some of the small clothes stores were having half-price sales. Maybe a nice scarf. No. It might be the wrong color or something. Donna was sort of picky about what she wore.

The hall ended at a big intersection called the Clock Court. In the center of the court stood a huge clock with giant Roman numerals. On the clock, just above the dial, there was a big castle carved out of wood and painted gold. The clock was chiming the hour as Susan approached.

There was a whirring sound and suddenly the gates of the castle opened and four little wooden knights on horseback came riding out. Two galloped around in a circle to the left, while the other two went to the right. Each time they passed each other, one of them was knocked back in the saddle by his enemy's lance.

Susan watched, fascinated, until the little knights finally disappeared once again into the castle courtyard and the gate closed behind them. All around her were murmurs of delight.

What a show! Susan thought. She'd definitely have to bring Howie here. He'd love it.

Leaving the Clock Court, she headed down a corridor that branched off the main passageway. There were smaller shops here. Specialty shops.

At the end of the hall was a little toy store.

Susan stopped and stared at it curiously. It looked different from the rest of the shops—almost as if it had been plucked from some other place and shoved into this hall. For one thing, it seemed older than the other stores. It was almost run-down. Its small windows were framed by dull wood that was chipped in places.

Susan peered inside, but the shop was too dimly lit for her to see anything. She looked up. A sign above the door proclaimed in old-fashioned, flowing script:

THE ONCE AND FOREVER TOY SHOP
JEREMY TIDWELL, PROPRIETOR

"Hmm," Susan said aloud. Should she go in? There *was* something strangely inviting about the

11

place. Maybe it was because it didn't seem as glitzy as the rest of the shops.

A little bell jangled as she opened the door.

Then she felt it again—that shivery feeling she'd had earlier.

What was the matter with her, anyway? Was she coming down with something?

And then she remembered what her father had said. About the goose walking on her grave. What did *that* mean? Whatever it was, it didn't sound very nice.

The shop was dark and deserted.

"Mr. Tidwell?" Susan called into the gloom. "Hello! Is anybody here?"

She sniffed once. The air smelled of must and mildew, like an old, abandoned attic.

The shop was actually a little bit creepy.

All the toys on the shelves looked old. There were little toy ships with real cloth sails. Dolls with painted china faces dressed in ruffles and holding little parasols. A doll-size set of blue willow china, laid out on a tiny table. And on the counter near the door stood a row of little tin soldiers.

Susan looked at the soldiers closely. They were shiny. Newly painted. But they looked . . . old.

Maybe it was their faces. They weren't the sort of faces you'd see on toys. These faces had set, angry expressions. Cruel, even.

One of the soldiers was holding a rifle with a bayonet. Susan had watched a lot of old war movies on TV. She remembered how she'd always get goose bumps when the commanding officer ordered, "Fix bayonets!"

The movies had always gotten gory at that point.

And here was a little toy soldier with—*oh no, how gross!* The toy manufacturer had painted the end of the bayonet red to look like blood.

Susan frowned.

The little soldier's leg was wrapped with a bandage that was splotched with red paint.

She brought her head even closer. The red paint almost looked like the real thing. It almost looked as if blood were oozing out of the bandage. Susan reached out her finger and touched the leg of the little figure.

Then she gasped.

The leg was warm and her finger came away wet. Without thinking, she put her finger in her mouth.

It tasted salty. And coppery.

Like blood.

And then a cold, clammy hand grabbed her shoulder.

Two

"May I show you something, my dear?" said a whispery voice. Susan choked back a scream and whirled, throwing off the hand.

A little old man stood smiling at her. He was wearing a formal, old-fashioned suit. Snow-white hair stuck out in tufts all over his head. His deep-set eyes were a pale, watery blue, the color of melting ice.

"No . . . no," Susan stammered, backing toward the door. She instantly forgot about the toy soldier. *A whole flock of geese must be walking over my grave right now,* she thought, judging by the cold chills she was feeling.

The old man continued to smile at her.

"I mean, I was just looking," Susan said, fumbling around behind her for the doorknob.

"Looking is always good," he said. His voice was soft, hypnotic. There was almost a lisp to it. And it had a singsong quality that made Susan feel drowsy and helpless.

He peered at her from under bushy white brows. "And I think I know exactly what it is you are looking for."

"You do?" Susan whispered back.

"It's right over here," he said gently, nodding his head. "Under that archway."

And then she saw it. It was framed by two velvet curtains, as if it were on a stage.

Her jaw fell open.

It was a dollhouse.

But this was no ordinary dollhouse. No, it was the most perfect, elegant, beautiful dollhouse Susan had ever seen.

She knew she had to leave. Her parents were waiting for her. She knew she had to walk out of the store this minute . . . but she couldn't. She couldn't bear to turn her back and walk away from that dollhouse.

Susan blinked, not believing her eyes. She'd often heard of love at first sight, but she'd always thought it had to do with something corny between grown-ups like her parents.

Now she knew better. Because that's how it was with her and the dollhouse. Love at first sight.

The little man was looking at her closely. "I'm right? That *is* what you were looking for, isn't it?"

"Oh yes," Susan said breathlessly. "Yes!"

The dollhouse stood on a long, low table. It was huge. It must have been at least three feet wide and three feet deep.

It had been built to look like an old-fashioned mansion—a Victorian mansion. The sort of house where there were maids and nannies.

The house was three stories high. It had a pointed roof, a wide front porch, and balconies on the second floor. The detail was amazing. The windows had real glass in them and the roof was made of tiny wooden shingles.

"Wow," Susan whispered.

Holding her breath, she took a step toward it.

Strangely enough, it was solid. Susan knew that most dollhouses were open in the back, so people could play with the furniture, but this one had four solid sides. A small room jutted out from the side of the first floor. The back left corner of the house had a little half-tower that extended up the entire house. A metal witch's hat roof topped the turret.

But the odd thing was that it looked so real.

"Nice, isn't it?" the man asked softly.

Susan nodded slowly. "Does it open?" she asked.

He smiled, then went up to it and pressed his fingers against one side. With a little *snick*, the back flipped up.

16

Susan leaned over and peered inside.

The dollhouse was completely empty. She put out a finger and gently touched one of the doors. It pushed open. She tried another, then another. All the doors worked and all the windows slid up and down.

"It's incredible," she murmured.

There was a stairway that led up from the front hall to the other floors, with a tiny, beautifully carved banister. The floor was made up of narrow little wooden floorboards.

The front door had a tiny, working brass knocker in the shape of an American eagle. And set in the outer wall, right where the staircase turned, was a little round stained-glass window that threw a colored pattern on the stairs.

Susan shook her head. Everything was so . . . *real*. It was almost as if someone could actually live here—someone tiny, like the people in *Gulliver's Travels*.

"But where's the furniture?" she asked.

"It hasn't come yet." He flashed her another strange smile. "I'm expecting it this afternoon."

Susan nodded. She wanted that dollhouse. More than that, she wanted to *live* in it, with its brass knocker and stained-glass window. She even knew what room she wanted—the little round

17

room with the high witch's hat roof on the second floor. It would be so much fun. She'd feel like a princess in a castle tower.

She closed her eyes and imagined herself walking through the tiny rooms. She knew she was being silly, but she couldn't help it. There was just something so perfect about that dollhouse . . .

When she opened her eyes, the old man was holding out a card.

"Please come visit me again," he said. "I am Jeremy Tidwell, the proprietor. I always enjoy people who appreciate my . . . ah . . . items."

Just then Susan glanced at a small antique carriage clock on a shelf.

She was late! Her parents were probably having fits!

"Susan! Where have you been!" her mother cried when Susan came dashing up to their meeting place.

"Oh, Mom, there was this toy store and—"

"Well, let's get going," her mother interrupted with a frown. "Dad and Howie are waiting for us in the car."

She took Susan by the elbow and steered her hastily toward the mall exit. "I don't want the movers to get there before us. We might find our furniture out on the lawn."

"I'm sorry, Mom. It's just that this dollhouse—"

"You shouldn't have worried us like that. We're in a strange place. I thought maybe something happened to you."

Susan opened her mouth again, then thought better of it. She *had* been late. But she couldn't have just walked away.

That dollhouse had been so wonderful—and yet so . . . well, *weird*.

Why had it affected her like that? It was almost as if it had cast a spell over her. Now that she was out of the shop, she could think clearly again. For some reason, her mind had been foggy back there. Maybe it was because the place had been so dark and musty and old-fashioned. She thought about all those weird toys and dolls. It had been like walking into the Twilight Zone or something!

And that weird little man, Mr. Tidwell. There was something creepy about him. That soft, whispery voice of his. Like a hypnotist's voice.

Had he hypnotized her?

Susan shook her head. Of course he hadn't! Things like that only happened in horror movies.

But as she left the mall, Susan found herself wishing she had never gone into The Once and Forever Toy Shop.

Three

"Well, here it is!" Susan's father exclaimed proudly.

Susan gasped.

She was sure she had lost her mind.

The house in front of her looked just like the dollhouse.

"Well, Susie, what do you think?" her father asked.

She couldn't answer. She stared at the house, frozen in the act of opening her car door, like someone in a game of Statues.

But there was no mistaking it. The house was *exactly* like the dollhouse. The wide front porch. The balconies on the second floor. The ornamental carving. The small room jutting out from the side on the first floor. The turret with its witch's hat roof.

And there, on the front door, was the American Eagle door knocker.

"Isn't that sweet, Henry?" Susan heard her mother say. Her voice seemed dim and muffled, as if it were coming from a far distance. "She's so carried away she can't even speak."

Mr. Martin unfastened his seat belt and opened his car door. "No wonder. How many kids her age get to live in a house like this?" He laughed. "I still don't know how I ever found it. It was just one of those once-in-a-lifetime lucky breaks, I guess. I tell you, Marion, it was almost as if the house picked *us*. As if it wanted us to live here."

Mrs. Martin crawled out of the car and looked around the yard. Her hands were clasped to her heart. "Those peony bushes are absolutely gorgeous, aren't they, Henry?" she cried. "And look at those climbing roses along the fence! We're going to love it here."

"Somebody does already," Mr. Martin said with a wink and a smile at his daughter.

Susan was standing on the sidewalk now, still unable to take her eyes away from the dreamlike vision in front of her. Was this house really hers? Hers to live in forever and ever?

It seemed only a few minutes had passed since she'd been in the toy shop, wishing she could live in the dollhouse. Wishing she could walk through its rooms. Wishing she could stand on the landing and watch the sun slanting in through the stained-glass window.

And now her wishes had come true.

But how could it be? How could the house look so much like the dollhouse?

Then Susan began to get a grip on herself. *Wait a minute.* Maybe it was the other way around. Maybe the dollhouse had been made to look like *this* house.

Of course. That had to be it.

Maybe the person who'd built the dollhouse had used this house as a model. Maybe the person had even lived here once, and had fallen in love with the place. Who wouldn't? Then maybe this same person had built a detailed replica of it— maybe for his or her children. And then somehow, over the years, the dollhouse had wound up in The Once and Forever Toy Shop.

That's how it must have happened. It all made perfect sense, now.

Suddenly Susan felt tremendously happy. She couldn't remember having ever felt this happy before.

Mrs. Martin put her hand on Susan's shoulder and gave her a little shake. "Earth to Susan. Earth to Susan. What do you say we go inside and pick out your new room?"

Susan looked at her mother, her eyes sparkling and her cheeks pink with excitement.

"I know exactly which one I want, Mom. The little round room on the second floor. The one in back."

"Of course, darling, if that's the one you—" Her mother stopped short. "But you haven't even seen the second floor yet. How did you . . . ?"

Susan was already on the porch, reaching for the doorknob. "This house is exactly like the dollhouse," she called. "The one at the mall."

She pulled the door open and laughed out loud.

Everything inside was exactly the same as the inside of the dollhouse, too.

There was the staircase, with the stained-glass window lighting up the landing. Even the banister was carved in the same design as the one in the dollhouse.

Whoever had built that model must have been good with his hands, Susan decided. It must have taken years!

She ran up the stairs, deliriously happy. And there, on the second floor, just down the hall, was the little circular room she had chosen for her own.

This was the room she had wished for. In the

house she had wished for. All her dreams were coming true!

Just then she heard the blast of a truck's horn out front. The movers had arrived.

After that, the house didn't look quite as much like the dollhouse anymore. Now it had furniture set haphazardly in the middle of rooms. Brown cardboard boxes were stacked everywhere, making it difficult to move around. Rolled-up carpets were propped here and there against the bare walls.

But Susan didn't care. She loved her new house and knew she was going to be happy there.

It was almost too perfect . . .

Four

Susan woke up the next morning with the sun streaming through the turret windows.

She looked up at her circular ceiling and smiled. She was in her room, her very own little room, just as she'd dreamed in the toy shop yesterday.

She glanced over at her bedside clock. The red numerals said 7:15.

Yawning, she pushed back the covers and swung her legs over the side of the bed. She felt for her slippers, then picked her way through the un-opened moving boxes that were strewn across her floor, heading for her dresser.

A glance in the bureau mirror told her that her hair was a mess, as usual.

Without even looking, she picked up her comb and ran it through her hair. But the comb felt strange and clunky. She held it out and looked at it.

It wasn't her comb. This comb was made of wood, with big, thick teeth.

"Where did this come from?" she said aloud.

Maybe it belonged to one of the moving men. That would make sense. And yet she couldn't remember any of them wearing dreadlocks or anything that would require a special comb like this.

Oh, well. There was no point in worrying about it. Right now she was in the mood for some breakfast.

Susan threw on her robe and started to open her bedroom door.

Just then a shadow fell across her room, as though the sun had been blocked out by a black cloud. She turned and looked toward the window.

What she saw made the blood drain from her face in terror.

An eye, a huge, blue human eye, was pressed against the window, looking in at her. It blinked.

Trembling, Susan backed against the door. She tried to scream, but nothing came out. She couldn't make a sound.

She tried again. Still nothing.

The enormous, staring eye backed away, and she saw a huge head with big tufts of white hair outside the window.

It was Jeremy Tidwell, the owner of the toy

shop! He was smiling, as if he could see her—as if he was pleased with what he saw.

I'm a doll, and this is a dollhouse, Susan thought frantically. *My wishes really* have *come true. I'm living in the dollhouse. And I'm trapped in here forever!*

Five

"Susan, wake up!" Mrs. Martin cried. "You're having a nightmare!"

Susan's eyes flew open. Her heart was pounding and she was damp with sweat.

Her mother was standing over her bed with a concerned look on her face.

Susan turned to the window. Nothing was out there but blue morning sky and sunshine. No staring eye. No huge head.

"I thought I'd get an early start," her mother said. "When I passed your room I heard you mumbling and shouting."

Susan let out a deep sigh. It had just been a bad dream—that was all. But it had seemed so real . . .

"It was more a morning mare than a nightmare, though, wasn't it?" her mom said, patting Susan's arm. "Well, I'd better get going. I've got to start opening boxes."

After her mom had shut the door behind her, Susan looked at the clock. The numerals read 7:20. It was now only five minutes later than it had been in her dream. Could it really have happened after all? Could she really have gotten up and seen that eye in the window? And then could she have gone back to bed and . . . No. She shook her head. That was silly.

Susan put on her slippers and stood. But she still felt a little shaky as she picked her way toward the bureau. What if the big wooden comb was really there?

It wasn't. Just her usual plastic comb and brush set.

She sighed again, feeling a little embarrassed about getting spooked. Everything was normal. Better than normal, even. Why wouldn't it be? Here she was, living in the greatest house in the world. She'd have to be pretty dumb not to appreciate that.

The sunshine streaming through the window lifted her spirits and she began to smile as she brushed her hair. There was no doubt about it— she was feeling better and better about this move all the time.

She'd sure miss Donna and the kids back home, though.

No, not home. She stopped brushing her hair and stared into her sleepy brown eyes in the mirror. She knew she couldn't call her old town "home" anymore. This was her home now.

And maybe she *would* meet some nice kids when she started school next week.

Hmm. The thought of facing a school yard full of strange faces made the pit of her stomach flutter. But she pushed the feeling aside, laid her brush down, and began rummaging through her bureau drawers.

After pulling on a pair of shorts and a T-shirt, she slipped her feet into her sneakers and went downstairs to breakfast.

The kitchen was a huge mess of unpacked boxes. Susan had to walk sideways, like a crab, to get to the table.

"It's going to take me all morning to organize this kitchen," Mrs. Martin said to nobody in particular. "It's a good thing there's a lot of cabinet space."

Mr. Martin was feeding Howie spoonfuls of mashed bananas. Howie was having fun, making a big show of chewing them and then squirting them back out. Runny banana was all over his plastic bib.

"You have three choices for breakfast this morning, Susan," her father said, patiently dabbing Howie's face and fat little neck with a paper napkin. "Cereal, cereal, or cereal."

Susan laughed. "I think I'll have the cereal."

"Sorry about that, but I haven't even found the toaster yet," Mrs. Martin said, bending over a box marked *CHINA*. "Tomorrow we'll have something a little more imaginative."

"Hey, Howie! How's it going?" Susan said, taking her place at the table.

Howie gave her an openmouthed smile that revealed new teeth and mashed bananas.

"Yuck," Susan said. "When will he start acting human, Dad?"

"I don't know." Her father grinned. "I'm still waiting for you to get there."

Clunk!

Susan jumped. Something had hit the floor behind her. She turned around to see her mother frowning.

"Darn it," Mrs. Martin said. "I dropped a plate. And it was one of the good china ones, too. The ones with the gold bands."

She knelt down and picked up three jagged shards of a dinner plate from the floor.

"Susan, would you please do me a favor and toss

31

these in the trash?" she asked, holding out the shards. "You can get at it better than I can. Be careful of the sharp edges, though."

"Sure, Mom." Susan took the pieces and carried them to the trash can in the corner. She started to throw them in but stopped and took a closer look at them. The broken edges looked dark and grainy.

"That's funny," she said. "This plate isn't china. It's made out of wood."

"Wood?" her father said, looking up from Howie's bananas. "No. Those plates are china. And good china at that."

Susan shrugged. "See for yourself." She held out a shard for her father's inspection and tapped a fingernail on it. It went *thud thud,* instead of *ping ping.*

A baffled expression came over Mr. Martin's face.

"Marion, come see this. Susan's right. This plate *is* made out of wood."

"How strange," Mrs. Martin said, taking one of the pieces. "I ought to write the manufacturer about this. Imagine selling wooden dishes and calling them china! Are they all like that?"

She took another plate, a smaller one this time, from the pile stacked on the countertop. While

Susan and her father watched, she rapped it gently against the side of the sink. A little piece cracked off the edge.

Mrs. Martin frowned. "This one's china, and now I've ruined a good plate."

She pulled the rest of the set out of the box, unwrapping each piece and examining it carefully before stacking it on the sink.

"The rest seem okay," she said. "But I'm *definitely* going to write the manufacturer and find out what's going on."

Mr. Martin wiped Howie down with a damp cloth and carried the gooey baby dish to the sink. "I think I'll start in on the basement, Marion. There's a wonderful old cabinet down there for my tools."

Susan tuned her parents' voices out as they made plans for the day. She dug into her cereal, chewing slowly and thinking.

Finding that wooden plate had been weird. It was just like that wooden comb thing in her dream.

What was happening around here, anyway?

Then she remembered the dollhouse. Dollhouse items—things like plates and bowls and little play telephones—were carved of wood, weren't they?

And their house looked like a dollhouse, so . . .

No! She shook her head so violently that Howie laughed and began to imitate her.

No, she told herself again. She was mixing it up. Her house didn't look like a dollhouse. A dollhouse looked like her house.

That made a difference. A big difference.

She wasn't living in a dollhouse. She was living in a real house. She had to stop imagining things before she drove herself nuts. So she had a nightmare. Big deal! Who didn't?

And, coincidentally, one of Mom's good plates turned out to be made of wood. The manufacturer would probably have a good explanation for that.

But still . . . what if everything in their house really *was* dollhouse furniture?

Six

Susan finished unpacking the boxes in her room that morning. It was hard to arrange things in a semicircular room. She only had one flat wall, which her bed and bureau were against.

She finally decided she'd go for a sort of free-floating, middle-of the-room arrangement for her chair, bookcase, and desk.

When she finished, she stepped back and admired the effect. The room looked neat and cozy.

Great. Now all she needed was a friend or two with whom to share it. Someone to come up here to talk to and trade secrets and giggle with.

Again she thought about starting at a new school next week and felt butterflies.

I'm sure it'll be fine, she told herself. *Won't it?*

*   *   *

During lunch, her mother declared she needed a break.

"I've been bent over, unpacking boxes all morning," she said with a sigh. "I need to walk upright for a change. I thought I'd go up to the mall and pick out curtains."

Susan was in the middle of wolfing down a peanut butter and jelly sandwich. She thought about the mall as she chewed. After waking up this morning, she hadn't wanted to see Mr. Tidwell again. Ever!

But now she wasn't so sure. Mr. Tidwell probably knew where the dollhouse had come from. Maybe he could tell her who had made it. And why.

She couldn't explain it, but since she had moved into the house, she'd felt kind of strange— almost as if someone were watching her. Maybe she wouldn't feel so uneasy if she knew more about the dollhouse. And maybe Mr. Tidwell could tell her something about *this* house. There had to be some kind of connection between the two.

She swallowed the mouthful of sandwich and washed it down with some milk. "Could I come along, Mom?"

"Since when are you interested in curtains, Susan?"

"Since never," Susan replied with a grin. "But there are some really neat stores up there."

Her mother raised an eyebrow. "You gave me a scare last time, remember? If I take you, do you promise to meet me promptly at the time we agree on?"

Susan crossed her heart with her finger. "Promptly. That's a promise."

The mall was packed. Susan and her mother parted at the entrance to the mall's biggest department store.

"Now remember—one hour. Okay?"

"Okay, Mom."

Susan stopped at the Bird Court to check the map.

The Bird Court was a noisy, colorful place with huge, wrought-iron cages containing exotic birds— parrots, parakeets, cockatoos, mynah birds. People stopped to admire the birds and tried to get them to talk.

Susan didn't care for that court. All the squawking gave her a headache. Besides, she was allergic to birds. They made her sneeze.

She walked quickly through the main hallway to the Clock Court, arriving just in time to see the little knights on their horses mark the hour by riding around and knocking each other down.

Finally she reached the little corridor that led to Mr. Tidwell's Once and Forever Toy Shop.

The little bell jangled as she opened the door.

The shop was dimly lit and deserted, just as it had been last time.

Strange, thought Susan. *Why isn't Mr. Tidwell ever in the front of the store, the way most shopkeepers are? Doesn't he have any other customers? There wasn't anyone in here last time, either.*

The thought gave her a creepy feeling. The cold, musty air in the shop made gooseflesh rise on her arms.

Suddenly she heard a noise behind her. She whipped around, expecting to see Mr. Tidwell.

Instead, she found herself looking into the faces of a row of old-fashioned dolls.

One of them seemed to be staring at her.

And then Susan was sure the doll winked and waggled a china head at her.

She moved closer, wanting to see if the doll would do it again. Was it a mechanical trick or something? But the doll only stared straight ahead, glassy-eyed and smiling.

Susan frowned. Her imagination was getting the best of her again. She looked at her watch. It had taken her longer to walk through the mall to get here than she'd realized. If Mr. Tidwell didn't show up soon, she'd have to leave.

But just then her eyes fell on the dollhouse.

She wasn't even aware of what she was doing as she walked over to the little archway, with its velvet curtains looped back like theater curtains.

All she could think was that the dollhouse was the most beautiful thing she had ever seen. It was almost as if it had called her to its side. A happy feeling came over her—a feeling of coming home to an old friend. She walked around the dollhouse carefully, drinking in every detail.

Wait a minute.

Something was different.

The dollhouse wasn't empty.

Looking through a window, Susan could see that little pieces of furniture were scattered through the rooms, as if they'd been left there by moving men. Tiny carpets were rolled up and leaning against walls. There were even little packing boxes, no bigger than matchbooks, stacked in every room.

It looked as if a miniature family had moved into the dollhouse and hadn't finished unpacking yet.

How weird! Why would Mr. Tidwell want to do something like that? It wasn't at all attractive.

And then she noticed something else. There were dolls in the house.

From what she could see, looking through the small window, there were four of them. Even though they were positioned with their backs to her, she could tell that they were a typical dollhouse family: a mother, a father, a girl, and a baby.

Eagerly, holding her breath, she fumbled around the side wall of the house, searching for the hidden spring that would open the back. At first she couldn't find it. Finally her fingers connected with what felt like a little flat button, and she pushed it.

The back popped open with a quiet click.

Susan smiled. Now she could really take a close look. Hunching down with her hands on her knees, she brought her head closer to the dollhouse.

And what she saw almost made her faint.

The furniture was her family's furniture! The dining-room table looked exactly like her parents' dining-room table—oval-shaped and made of shiny brown oak. It even had the same folding flaps on the ends that could be used to extend it. And the blue-and-white-striped fabric on the chairs was the exact same pattern and color as the fabric on the chairs at home.

Frantically, not believing her eyes, she went through the rooms, pushing the tiny cardboard boxes aside with a fingertip so she could see the pieces of furniture behind them.

Susan's heart began beating faster.

Every dresser, chair, table, and bed in the doll-house mirrored one in Susan's real house. Everything matched the furniture in the Martin house.

Not close. Not almost. *Exactly.*

Except for one thing. On the bureau of the little turret room on the second floor, there was a small carved wooden comb. It didn't look like Susan's regular comb.

Susan gasped.

It looked just like the comb in her dream!

She leaned in closer. Her heart was beating so fast now she thought it was going to leap out of her throat. With trembling fingers, she turned the dollhouse family dolls around so she could see them.

She bit her lip to keep from screaming.

They looked like her family—her *real* family.

And the girl doll looked just like her!

Seven

"The furniture came in," said a soft, whispery voice at her shoulder.

Susan spun around. It was Mr. Tidwell. He had a secretive, excited look about him. His white hair stood up even more wildly around his head than it had the last time she'd seen him.

She stared at him with wide, frightened eyes—but he didn't seem to notice. He smiled.

"It will take a while before it's really homey, don't you think?" he said gently, pointing to the scattered furniture and stacked boxes.

"Mr. Tidwell," Susan began. Her mouth was so dry that she could hardly get the words out. "The furniture . . . that furniture is just like . . ."

"So many things have to be done," he continued, shifting the tiny pieces of furniture around. "The unpacking. Putting things in their proper places."

"But, that furniture and those—"

"You know," Mr. Tidwell went on, as if he didn't hear her, "it takes a lot to make a house a home, doesn't it? It takes people."

He flashed Susan a quick crooked-toothed grin, then set the mother doll on the living-room couch.

The doll was made out of flexible wires, so he could arrange the small limbs. He stretched the mother out in an attitude of fatigue—arms flung out, legs extended.

Susan just stood there, gaping at the doll in disbelief. The mother doll looked exactly like Susan's mom. She had short, ash-blond hair and tiny painted blue eyes. She was even wearing the same color slacks and style of top Mrs. Martin had put on to come shopping at the mall!

Then he took the father doll and placed a cardboard box in his hands, bending the small wire hands to hold it. The father doll, with its painted salt-and-pepper gray hair and khaki slacks, looked just like Mr. Martin. And what's more, he was wearing a tool belt, the way Susan's father had been that morning when he'd gone downstairs to work in the basement.

The baby doll was in his playpen. Howie!

Oh, no. Not little Howie.

Susan reached out and grabbed Mr. Tidwell's

43

arm. "Mr. Tidwell. You've got to tell me what's going on around here."

The old shopkeeper merely picked up the sister doll and held it up before her eyes. It had brown hair down past its shoulders, brown eyes, and dimples—just like Susan.

Susan began to feel sick.

"She looks like me," she whispered.

"Do you think so?" he asked. "I call her Susan. Isn't that a pretty name for her?"

"But . . . but that's my name."

All of a sudden Susan wasn't looking at the doll anymore. She was looking into Mr. Tidwell's eyes. And not being able to look away. Not being able to escape those watery blue depths.

And not wanting to.

Mr. Tidwell continued talking. Susan wasn't really aware of what he was saying. Something about relaxing and putting herself into his hands. Trusting him. Things like that.

All she knew was that the more he spoke, the less she began to worry about the dollhouse. About the furniture looking just like the furniture in her real house.

About the little dolls that looked just like herself and her family.

Mr. Tidwell's voice soothed on. It was the warmest,

nicest, most comforting voice she had ever heard.

Then he smiled, and suddenly she felt very happy, as happy as she'd felt yesterday when she'd first seen the dollhouse.

She smiled back at him, feeling as if she'd just awakened from a lovely, lovely dream.

"This dollhouse has been here for a long, long time," he said.

Susan nodded, trying to remember the questions she had meant to ask him. She knew she'd come here to find out something about the dollhouse. But what?

"Stay here as long as you like," Mr. Tidwell said. "The dollhouse likes you."

With a final wispy smile, he floated away toward another section of the store.

Susan bent over the house again. It no longer surprised her to see that the furniture in the dollhouse was exactly like hers at home. Or that the little dolls resembled her family.

All she knew was that she loved that dollhouse.

And that she wanted it for her very own.

Eight

Susan could have stayed there all day, playing with the dollhouse. But a look at her watch sent her scurrying. She was supposed to meet her mother in just a few minutes. She couldn't afford to be late again.

Before she left the toy shop, she cast a quick glance at the row of dolls by the door. Her eyes fell on the one who she thought had winked at her when she had first walked in.

The doll, with its long chestnut curls and red satin dress, seemed to be staring at her again.

Well, of course she is, Susan told herself sensibly. *That's how her glass eyes are set in her head.*

And yet the doll's look seemed to hold a secret. It was almost as if she knew something Susan didn't. Something that gave her great pleasure.

Something evil.

Susan swallowed as she opened the door to leave. The little bell tinkled, and she felt a cold shudder run down her spine—the way it had yesterday, when she'd first entered The Once and Forever Toy Shop.

She frowned. Something *evil*? What was the matter with her, anyway? How could she think such crazy, far-out thoughts about a harmless little china doll?

Standing in the doorway, Susan took a last look back at the store. Mr. Tidwell was nowhere in sight, as usual. She looked over at the counter, where the little tin soldiers had been yesterday. They weren't there now. She wondered what had happened to them, especially the one with the bandaged leg. Had they gone back to war?

She shook her head in disgust. *Gone to war*? What was her problem?

She couldn't believe herself. She was usually so calm and levelheaded.

But the soldier's leg . . . that bloody bandage.

Susan closed the door to the shop quietly behind her and the bell jangled one last time.

Once she was out in the mall, among all the other shoppers, she could think more clearly. She felt as if she was awakening from a dream. And as she raced through the halls, all she could think about was how she wanted that dollhouse more than anything in the world.

But how could she get it? She had only a few dollars in her piggy bank. She never seemed to be able to save anything from her allowance. Would her parents buy it for her, maybe? Her birthday was only a couple of months away . . .

No. It was probably much too expensive. And they'd spent most of their savings on the down payment on the house and the move. Her parents had already told her that birthdays and Christmas would have to be scaled down this year.

Susan was panting by the time she reached her mother in front of the department store.

"Did you have a good time, Sweetie?" Mrs. Martin asked. She shifted her shopping bag to the other arm and pulled her big leather pouch back up on her shoulder.

"Yeah. Listen, Mom—you know that dollhouse I told you about? Can you come look at it now?"

Mrs. Martin sighed. "Could we do it another time, Susan? I'm really tired and I'd love to get home."

"Okay," Susan said, unable to keep the disappointment out of her voice.

She'd been hoping that if her mother saw the dollhouse, she might fall in love with it, too. And then maybe she might come up with the idea of buying it on her own, without having to be asked.

A wild shot, but there was no harm in trying.

"So where are the curtains?" Susan asked, pushing through the big glass exit door and holding it open for her mother.

Mrs. Martin didn't answer. She was busy scanning the parking lot. Susan rolled her eyes. Her mother was always forgetting where she parked.

"What? Oh, I only picked out the fabric and style, and gave them the measurements," she explained. "It'll be a few days before they're ready. But in the meantime, I got these nice thick towels on sale."

They had to wander up and down a few parking aisles before they finally located the car.

"Next car I get is going to be a flaming-orange convertible," Mrs. Martin said. "Everyone in the world must own a dark-gray hatchback like ours."

"Hey, Mom," Susan said as they pulled out of the parking lot. "It's going to be real easy to get to the mall from our house. I can take my bike and—"

Mrs. Martin flashed Susan a stern, sideways look. "Not by yourself, young lady. With me, fine. Or maybe with a couple of kids your age—careful, responsible kids, that is."

Susan stared out the window. Every now and then she really missed Donna. Now was one of those times. Here was this really great mall and she didn't have anyone to share it with!

"Mom," she said, going back to the subject that was most on her mind. "You really should see the dollhouse sometime. It isn't just a toy. It's a work of art."

Mrs. Martin looked amused. "Oh, I see. We're talking culture here, not just something to play with."

"Right! But there's more," Susan said.

"Uh-oh. What?"

"It looks exactly like our house."

"You mean it's a three-story Victorian?" Mrs. Martin asked absently.

"Yeah. But Mom—I mean it's *exactly* like ours."

She could tell her mother thought she was exaggerating, so she hurried on. "All the furniture, too. Even all the dolls that go with it. They look like us. There's one like you, one like Dad. The sister doll looks like me. And, Mom, the baby doll is just like Howie!"

Mrs. Martin turned into the driveway and eased the car to a stop. "My goodness," she said good-humoredly. "Not another Howie!"

Susan unfastened her seat belt. Maybe she

should stop hinting and cut right to the heart of the matter.

"Listen, Mom. I know that dollhouse is really expensive and all, but do you think . . . maybe for my birthday and Christmas . . . ?"

Her mother looked at her with a serious expression. "I really don't know, honey," she said slowly. "I guess it would depend on how much it costs. You know money's a little tight right now."

"I know," said Susan, getting out of the car. "But maybe you could go and look at it, just in case."

"Well, okay," her mother said.

"Thanks!" Susan cried happily, running up the driveway to the front porch of the big, beautiful house.

Nine

Monday was the first day of school.

The first day of a *new* school.

Susan wondered what the girls in her class would be wearing. Would they dress up? Or would they wear jeans or shorts?

She decided to play it safe, and wore a red-and-white-striped top with a short blue denim skirt that zipped up the front.

"Do you want me to drive you since it's your first day?" her mother asked. Susan noticed that her mom seemed almost as nervous as she was. "I mean, so you don't get lost or anything."

"Plee-eeese, Mom, don't drive me or come cruising by to make sure I got there all right," said Susan. "I don't want these kids to think I'm a baby!"

As Susan started off down the walk, she thought

about how it would be if she were still back in her old hometown. She'd be walking with Donna, and waving to everybody and talking about how she spent the summer.

She'd always felt sorry for the new kids at the start of school. She'd never been a new kid before. Now that she was in sixth grade, she knew it was going to be hard.

How on earth would she get through this day? She almost wished she were sick with a fever or something, so she could stay home.

Then she sighed. But what good would that do? She'd only have to face it when she got well.

A couple of boys her age bicycled past her. They acted just like she was invisible. Well, that was good. Sometimes boys could be awfully mean.

Two little seven- or eight-year-old girls came toward her when she reached the street that led to the school. There seemed to be a lot of kids walking toward school from her neighborhood. The little girls smiled shyly and Susan smiled back.

They must think I'm cool, Susan thought.

The thought made her feel a lot braver.

When she got to school, she headed straight for the principal's office.

The principal was out on the school grounds, but his secretary was behind her desk in the outer office. A brass nameplate on her desk told Susan that the secretary's name was Mrs. Jurgens.

Mrs. Jurgens was an older woman—older than Susan's mother—with glasses that went up at the corner like cats' eyes and a lot of red hair that she wore piled high on her head.

She seemed very nice.

"Here is your class schedule, Susan. I know it will be confusing at first, but you'll soon settle in. Your homeroom is right down that hall."

Susan's homeroom teacher was Mrs. Redding. She seemed nice, too. The first thing she did was give the kids a little speech on what would be expected of them this year, since they were now in the sixth grade.

Susan glanced nervously around the room. Most of the students seemed to know one another. A little lump came to her throat when she heard them talking and laughing about last year and all the things they'd done together.

She wondered if she could make it through the day without crying.

A couple of the girls smiled at her. At least that was a good sign. She tried to imagine what it would be like at a slumber party with them. That thin blonde one looked like fun. She kept all the others laughing.

One of the boys kept staring at Susan until his friend punched him in the arm and whispered something. He blushed and looked away.

Susan stole a look at him from behind her new notebook. He was kind of cute, with curly brown hair. His name was Mark. She'd heard the other boys call him that.

She'd planned to call Donna tonight, just to compare notes with her on schools. This would be something exciting to tell her. Donna would make a big romance out of it. Maybe this school wouldn't be so bad after all.

The new school was a little bigger than her old school, so she kept turning down wrong hallways and blundering into wrong rooms until she got the hang of how everything was laid out. She wished they had a big map in the entrance hall, the way they did at the mall.

The mall!

She'd almost forgotten about it. And the dollhouse.

How could she, when the dollhouse was the most important thing in her life? She wished she could remember what Mr. Tidwell had said to her about it, though, when she was staring into his eyes. She thought and thought about it all morning long. Finally she remembered something vague—something about not being frightened because the furniture in the dollhouse looked just like her own and that the dolls looked just like her family.

What a funny thing to say, Susan thought. Of course she wasn't frightened! It was only logical that if a house looked like your house, the furniture and people inside would look the same, too.

Wasn't it?

Or did she think that just because Mr. Tidwell had told her to think it?

Art class was at two o'clock. Susan liked art. She hoped they would be doing some fun projects this year.

The art room was on the first floor. It was big and sunny, with several large worktables instead of desks. Susan took a seat across the table from the thin blond girl she'd seen that morning in homeroom.

The teacher, Mrs. West, handed out blocks of clay. "After a long first day back at school, I think it's time we got our hands dirty, don't you?" she asked, smiling. "Just squish it between your fingers to soften it up. And then make the first thing that comes to your mind."

"I'm going to make a big snake," said one of the boys.

"Some artist, Josh!" the blond girl said.

As Susan sat pounding clay in her hands, she thought once again about the dollhouse and how wonderful it would be to own it. To have it for her very own.

She rolled her clay out and, to her surprise, found herself building a little house.

She made a floor, then four walls, like a clay box. Then she added a curved turret in one corner. The balconies and the porch would be harder. She would have to roll out a lot of pieces into thin, long strings.

She leaned back in her chair a little to look at her clay house. The blond girl was watching her.

Her hair was long and pulled back with barrettes. She was wearing jeans and a baggy black T-shirt with a big silver eye painted on it. Susan admired the way she carried off the cool, casual look.

"What are you making?" Susan asked the girl, who'd been pushing her clay around, lumping it together and then breaking it down again.

"Nothing, really," the girl replied with a little smile. "I'm just getting a feel for it. I like clay."

Susan nodded. "Me, too."

"What are you making?"

"A house," Susan told her. She didn't want to

confess that she was making a little clay *dollhouse*.

"I'm Kelly," the other girl said. "Kelly Stockton. I guess you're new here, huh?"

"Yeah. We just moved in. I'm Susan Martin."

As they talked, the girls realized they would be having three classes together—and that their lunch periods were the same.

"I'll introduce you around tomorrow," Kelly said. "It's not that big a school. In a couple of days, you'll know just about everybody."

Josh poked Kelly's arm with the head of his clay snake, making hissing sounds.

Kelly rolled her eyes. "And some you'll wish you didn't!"

She pushed Josh's snake away with one hand while she asked, "Where do you live?"

"We just moved into that big old house on the corner of Pine Street," Susan answered. "The one with the turret. Do you know which one I mean?"

Kelly stopped squeezing her clay and her eyes suddenly lit up. "You're kidding!" she exclaimed. "I've always wondered about that place. It's so big and beautiful." She smiled. "You're really lucky."

"Yeah." Susan smiled back. "It's pretty nice."

"Now that I know someone who lives there, I have an excuse to come check it out," Kelly added with a sly little grin.

Susan looked back at the little clay house she was making. She *was* pretty lucky, she had to admit. But still, something wasn't quite right. She wasn't any closer to finding out who had built the dollhouse. Or why. . . .

On her way home, Susan decided that she liked her new school. The kids all seemed pretty nice, and her classes were fun. Best of all, it took her mind off the dollhouse.

Until the following week.

The following week, things at home started to turn into wood.

Nobody could figure out what was happening.

The first item was the new extension telephone that Mrs. Martin took out of the box.

"What is this?" she cried. "A model or something? This phone is carved out of wood!"

The second was the antique Chinese bowl that Great-Aunt Tilly had given Mr. and Mrs. Martin for a wedding present.

"I can't believe this is the same bowl we've had for fifteen years!" Mrs. Martin wailed. "Those movers must have some sort of crooked scam going on. I'm going to put the insurance people on this one. It was a family heirloom. Believe me, heads will roll!"

Then Susan found a wooden brush and comb on her dresser, just as she had in her dream.

When she saw them, she looked quickly out the turret window, expecting to see a huge, watery eye peering in on her.

There was nothing out there but blue sky.

But for strange reason, she couldn't bring herself to tell her parents about what had happened. Too many crazy things were going on already, she reasoned. They had enough to worry about.

Then Howie's plastic baby seat was suddenly discovered to be made of wood.

"Am I losing my mind, or what?" asked Mrs. Martin, throwing her arms out dramatically. "Will someone please tell me what's happening around here?"

Susan was afraid she knew the answer.

The house was turning into the dollhouse.

Ten

Susan needed someone to talk to, but she didn't know who.

She'd called Donna, and they'd had a good time giggling together, but everything was changed now. Susan knew she would probably never go back to her old home, except maybe for a visit, so things and people there just weren't as important to her now as they had been three weeks ago.

And what good would it do to try to tell Donna about what was happening here? Donna might think she was making it all up. Or that she'd gone out of her mind.

So what about Kelly?

Susan had discovered that Kelly lived only a couple of blocks from her house. They'd been walking to school together every day for a week. Kelly had introduced her to all the kids at school, and she was even invited to a Saturday-night slumber party.

And Mark—the boy with the curly hair, who'd stared at her the first day of school—was still staring. Susan figured it was time for one of them to smile at the other. Should she go first? She'd have to ask everybody at the Saturday-night slumber party.

All in all, she was settling in nicely at school.

But the house was something else.

Would Kelly believe her when she told her that everything was turning to wood?

As the days passed, Susan's memory of Mr. Tidwell had begun to dim. She was beginning to forget the things he had told her as she stared into his eyes.

But she had begun to wonder more and more about the furniture that looked exactly like the pieces in her own home.

And about the four dolls that looked like her family.

They didn't seem as normal or natural to her now as they had after Mr. Tidwell had spoken to her about them in that soft, whispery voice.

So on Wednesday when Kelly asked if she wanted to go to the mall with her after school the next day, she eagerly accepted.

She'd take Kelly to Mr. Tidwell's Once and Forever Toy Shop and see what she thought. Kelly had a lot of common sense. Maybe she'd be able to help.

The girls bicycled to school the next day, so they could get to the mall and home again without having to call one of their mothers.

"The Once and Forever Toy Shop?" Kelly asked curiously. "That really run-down-looking place near the Clock Court?"

"Yeah," Susan replied. "Have you ever been inside?"

Kelly shook her head. "No. It always looks so dark and empty." She paused and looked at Susan. "To be honest, that place has always sort of given me the creeps."

As usual, the little bell jangled as they opened the door into Mr. Tidwell's dimly lit shop. And, as usual, Mr. Tidwell was nowhere to be seen.

Susan wondered where he was. He always seemed to pop out from nowhere. It was downright spooky.

"Wow," Kelly whispered. "This store is pretty . . . different."

The row of china dolls stared at them from their place on the shelf. The tin soldiers were still nowhere in sight, but there was another set of soldiers on the counter. These were modern looking, and wore beige camouflage uniforms. The soldiers looked tired and grimy, as if they'd just come from the desert.

"Look at this," Kelly said, picking something off a shelf. "Can you believe it? It looks like something right out of the Addams family."

She held up a cast-iron bank in the shape of a guillotine, with a victim kneeling in front of it, his head in a groove under the blade.

"This thing is really sick," Kelly said.

Nevertheless, she set the bank on the counter and fished around in her pocket for a nickel.

She put the nickel in a little slot on the side of the guillotine and pressed a lever.

The guillotine blade dropped down and lopped off the victim's head, while the nickel disappeared inside the bank.

The victim's head rolled into a little metal basket.

Kelly picked up the man's head and snapped it back into place.

"Eeewh! Who'd ever buy something like this for a little kid?" she asked. "Whatever happened to piggy banks?"

She pushed it back on the counter, behind another toy, as if that would get rid of it.

"This store has some pretty unusual things," Susan agreed shakily.

"What else have they got here?" Kelly asked with a crooked grin. "Toy atom bombs?"

Then Kelly's eyes drifted past Susan. A sudden look of fear came over her face. "What's that?" she asked, staring.

ELEVEN

Susan spun around quickly, half expecting to see a murderous toy in action. Or a doll winking and nodding with an evil smile. Or even Mr. Tidwell . . .

There was nothing.

Nothing except the dollhouse, sitting on its table in the archway.

"That's your house," Kelly said in a low, nervous voice. "That's an exact model of your house."

"I know," Susan said. "It's beautiful, isn't it?" She watched Kelly closely for her reaction.

Kelly looked at her oddly. "You don't think it's weird that there's a model of your house in this creepy store?"

"We-ell, maybe at first," Susan said slowly. "Yes, I guess so. But then I figured it all out."

She took a deep breath and continued, "See, maybe the builder of the house made that model.

Or somebody who lived there and loved the house as much as I do made it and . . ."

Her voice trailed away and she locked eyes with Kelly.

"Somebody who loved the house?" repeated Kelly in a low voice. "Susan, whoever made that model must have *really* loved the house. I mean, it's almost kind of scary . . ."

Susan began to feel a little dizzy. "What do you mean?" she whispered.

"I mean it's—" Kelly broke off suddenly with a nervous little laugh. "I'm sorry, Susan. I didn't mean to get you all worked up. I have this problem, see? It's my out-of-control imagination. I'm always making up stories in my mind and scaring myself half to death. You're right. The builder probably made this model."

"But Kelly—"

"Now let's see this thing up close," Kelly said.

Susan frowned.

Kelly walked over to the dollhouse, bent down, and put her eye to one of the windows.

Susan could tell that Kelly was being extra enthusiastic for her sake.

"Wow!" said Kelly. "Everything sure looks real in there. There's even a lot of cute little pieces of furniture."

67

"Wait a minute," Susan said. "The back comes up."

She went over to the dollhouse and felt around on the side for the button. The back popped up smoothly when she pressed it.

"That's funny," she said. "The furniture's all arranged and the packing boxes are gone."

She looked into one room after the other. Just as before, all the furniture was the same as the furniture in the Martin home. But now the boxes were all unpacked. The rugs were rolled out. And the furniture was arranged in the exact same way as it was at home.

That feeling of dizziness came over her again—only this time, much, much stronger.

Someone's been spying on us, Susan thought. *Someone's been watching our house. How else could this have happened?*

"Susan? Are you okay?" Kelly turned toward her and, as she did, she accidentally knocked a small red pot of tiny, artificial geraniums off the dollhouse porch. It fell to the ground with a clatter.

She hurriedly picked it up and replaced it.

"Are you okay?" Kelly said again. "You look so funny. Kind of greenish."

"Kelly," Susan said. "I want you to look at the dolls in that house and tell me what you think."

Kelly stuck her head in the house and pulled out the first doll she could find. She held it up with a smile. "This one looks like you," she said.

Suddenly Susan felt faint.

Suddenly the dollhouse was beginning to worry her. Really worry her.

Before, her thoughts about the dollhouse had been dreamy and happy.

Wait a minute. That was after Mr. Tidwell had looked in her eyes and told her all those things that she couldn't remember.

Had he hypnotized her?

And if he had—why?

Susan looked back and forth between the dollhouse and Kelly. She knew now that if she didn't tell someone about all the strange things that had been happening in connection with the dollhouse, she would burst.

She hadn't known Kelly long. Just a week. But she had the feeling that Kelly was a true friend, and could be trusted. And more than that, Kelly was smart and sensible. She'd know what to think of all this.

"Kelly," she said, her voice quavering. "That doll *is* me."

Twelve

Kelly looked at Susan, then back at the doll.

"What do you mean?" she asked, as if she wasn't sure whether or not Susan was kidding.

Susan didn't know quite how to begin. "That's the sister doll," she said. "See, she's even got dimples, just like me. And that outfit she's wearing? That's what I had on the first day I came into this store."

Then she reached into the dollhouse and brought out the other dolls.

"Here's the mother doll. She looks exactly like my mother. Blond hair. Blue eyes. Everything. And this is my father. Another perfect match. And the baby is my brother, Howie."

She set the dolls down beside the dollhouse.

"They look like my family," she said. "They don't sort of look like them. They look like them exactly."

"Could it be a coincidence?" Kelly asked slowly, looking at the sister doll again. "I mean, these dolls are really small, Susan. You can't get too much detail on them."

Susan shook her head. Her brown hair swung from side to side. "No, it definitely isn't a coincidence. Those dolls are even wearing clothes that match ours. And the father doll has a tool belt around his waist, just like my dad's."

She waited for Kelly's reaction, but Kelly only stared at her.

"And that's not all," Susan went on. "The furniture is like our furniture at home. We have an Oriental rug just like this. And that's our dining-room table. And I have furniture in my room that matches the things in the turret bedroom."

Kelly looked where she was pointing. "Is there anything that isn't the same?"

Susan examined the dollhouse closely. Yes, there was something different, but what was it?

"The curtains are new," said a familiar whispery voice behind them.

Both girls jumped and turned.

How does he do that? Susan wondered. *How does he always seem to appear out of nowhere?*

Mr. Tidwell was wearing the same antique-looking dark suit he'd been wearing the last time.

71

It was like something out of an old photo, Susan thought. The lapels were funny and the shoulders were slightly pinched. His shirt collar was high and rounded.

As Susan uneasily introduced him to Kelly, she noticed that his white hair was sticking up more wildly than it had been last time. Even his white eyebrows looked longer and bushier.

Susan's heart was pounding.

But as soon as she heard his voice, she began to grow calmer.

He had such a lovely, soothing voice.

She could just listen to that voice and . . .

No! That's what had happened both times she'd come in here. Something about that voice made her forget things.

She looked over at Kelly. Kelly was listening to Mr. Tidwell, too, with a strange, dreamy look on her face.

Susan coughed loudly and bumped into Kelly, rousing her. "What were you saying about the curtains?" she asked crisply.

Mr. Tidwell gestured to the windows. "We have new curtains," he repeated. "Do you like them?"

Susan looked. Sure enough, there were new drapes in the living room. They were blue, with tiny, tasseled gold tiebacks.

The dining room had white lace curtains in the windows. Even the pattern of the lace was miniature. Susan wondered who could have made something that small and fine.

The rest of the house was curtained, too. There were bright yellow ones in the master bedroom. Fringed pink in the turret room. Short cafe curtains in the nursery, with tiny little balloons on them.

Susan's house on Pine Street didn't have curtains yet.

It was only a small difference, but it made her feel better somehow.

"Are they like the ones in your house?" Kelly whispered in Susan's ear, so Mr. Tidwell wouldn't hear.

"No," Susan said. "Except for the curtains, though, it's all the same."

She rubbed her hands over her forearms, and found they were covered with goose bumps.

Mr. Tidwell stroked the roof of the dollhouse, humming a tuneless little song. Humming and stroking, humming and stroking. Almost as if the dollhouse were his pet.

Kelly and Susan exchanged glances. Susan knew exactly what Kelly was thinking.

That there was something very, very wrong with Mr. Tidwell.

Kelly suddenly looked at her watch.

"Nice meeting you, Mr. Tidwell. I have to go home, now. My mother's waiting for me."

She elbowed Susan sharply.

"Oh, uh, yes," Susan put in. "I have to go, too."

As they bicycled home, Kelly asked, "Do you think I could stop by your house and use your phone? I have to call my mom."

"Sure," Susan said. "You're not afraid of coming in, are you? Because of . . . you know . . . the dollhouse?"

"If it doesn't scare you, it doesn't scare me," Kelly said, her blond hair flying out behind her as she pedaled faster.

Susan stood up and pumped her pedals, too. She was happy she wasn't all alone now, facing this strange thing that was happening to her. Somehow having Kelly made her feel safer.

Kelly could pedal faster than Susan and she knew the streets better. She seemed to know exactly how to get to Susan's house.

Finally they turned onto Pine Street. There, up ahead, was Susan's house. They started to cross the street toward it. Then suddenly they both stopped, right in the middle of the road.

Susan looked at her house and then at Kelly.

There were curtains in the windows. They could see them from here. Blue drapes in the living room. White curtains in the dining room. And upstairs, in the windows of the big bedroom at the front of the house, were cheerful yellow ones.

Kelly eyed Susan suspiciously. "This isn't a joke, is it?" she asked. "You're not putting me on or something, are you?"

"No. Believe me, Kelly. This is no joke. I wish it were."

Just then Mrs. Martin came out on the porch. Susan waved to let her know she was home. Her mother waved back, and accidentally knocked over a red pot of geraniums. Before she could catch it, it rolled down the stairs and out on the pavement.

Kelly gasped. Susan bit her lip. The pot of geraniums looked exactly like the miniature ones Kelly had knocked over on the dollhouse porch.

"Come on in," Mrs. Martin called out as she picked up the flowers and put them back on the porch. "Our curtains just came today. The place looks like a real home now."

"So now, I guess everything *does* match exactly," Susan said hopelessly.

Thirteen

That night, Susan had another nightmare.

She dreamed she was in her room and had just woken up. The room was full of sunshine. For some reason, she hadn't closed her curtains the night before. Her windows were open, too, and she could hear birds chattering in the big oak tree in the driveway.

Getting out of bed, she shuffled over to her bureau. She pulled on the handle of the top drawer, but the drawer wouldn't open.

None of the other ones would, either. They were stuck shut. No, they were made like that. The bureau was a big hunk of solid, carved wood, like the toy bureau in the dollhouse.

Then a shadow fell across the room.

Startled, she wheeled around to see a huge human eye, a watery blue eye, peering into her room.

It was just like last time. She tried to scream, but nothing came out. She backed against her door, fumbling for the knob.

Then a huge hand came through the window. A human hand, covered with pale, wrinkled skin.

The hand groped around blindly, its fingers opening and closing, as if searching for her.

Yanking her bedroom door open, Susan fled into the hall. The hall looked so long. And so dark.

Finally she reached its end and burst into her mother's room. Mrs. Martin was sitting at her makeup table, dressed in her pink bathrobe.

"Mom! Mom!" Susan managed to gasp. "Help me!"

She grabbed her mother's shoulder but, to her horror, Mrs. Martin fell sideways off the bench.

She was a huge doll—the mother doll from the dollhouse.

The doll lay stiffly on the floor, its painted blue eyes staring sightlessly at the ceiling.

Then the sun in that room was blotted out, too.

Slowly, Susan turned. There it was. The big blue eye. The old hand.

It started to come through this window, too . . .

"Susan! Susan! Wake up," said a voice.

Her mother was holding her, comforting her.

She was flesh and blood, not a doll. Susan had to touch her, just to make sure she was real.

That's it! Susan decided right then and there. *I'm gonna do something about this dollhouse once and for all.*

Susan was waiting for Kelly at her locker when the final bell rang that day at school.

"Kelly," she said urgently before Kelly even had a chance to say hello. "Do you want to go with me to the mall this afternoon? I have to take another look at that dollhouse."

Kelly looked puzzled. "You're sure you want to go back to the mall?"

Susan shook her head. "No. I'd really rather not. But I feel like I have to."

They left school and headed down Hill Street.

"How come?" Kelly asked. "I thought you decided not to go there anymore."

"I had this nightmare last night," explained Susan. "It was so real. And Mr. Tidwell was in it."

Kelly nodded thoughtfully. "So you're facing your fears, is that it?"

"Sort of." She glanced at her friend. "Thanks a lot for coming with me, Kelly."

"No problem," said Kelly airily. "What are friends for?"

Ahead of them was the mall, its huge white walls and glass windows sparkling in the afternoon sun. But Susan noticed some heavy gray clouds drifting in. She shivered a little, in spite of the day's warmth.

"I'm not even sure what I expect to find there," she said.

"Maybe it will be something nice," Kelly said cheerfully. "What if one of the dolls has found a lost treasure in the attic? And now all the dolls are filthy rich. Maybe this time there'll be a miniature red Ferrari parked outside the dollhouse."

Susan had to laugh. Then she had a frightening thought. "What if Mr. Tidwell sold the dollhouse?"

"Your troubles would be over, Susan. You wouldn't have to worry about it anymore."

"I don't know," she said doubtfully. "Those little dolls are *us*. I'd hate to have some mean little kid playing with them."

She walked a little faster, and soon they were in the mall and hurrying through its corridors.

Then Kelly and she were pushing open the door to The Once and Forever Toy Shop.

"Doesn't anyone ever come in here besides us?" Kelly whispered. "This must be the most deserted place in the world."

"I don't know where Mr. Tidwell hides out,

either," Susan whispered back. "He's never around, and then he just suddenly appears."

Staying close together, the two girls walked over to the dollhouse. Susan popped the back open and they looked inside.

"It looks just the same," Kelly said softly. "Too bad there's no Ferrari in the driveway."

"Well, those are the breaks." Susan bent down to examine each floor carefully.

The baby doll was in his playpen in the living room. The father doll was missing, though.

Does he go off to work, just like Dad does? Susan wondered.

She looked for the sister doll. She was on her bed in the turret room. Susan's eyes widened. Something was wrong. Someone had posed the doll to look frightened and upset. Her hands were raised to the sides of her face, as if she were alarmed about something.

Susan's heart began to pound. What had happened? Why was the doll looking so frightened?

"Look over here, Susan." Kelly's voice was tense. "Here by the stairs."

On the first floor, the mother doll lay at the bottom of the stairs, as though she had fallen. One leg was twisted unnaturally, and one arm was up, as if calling for help.

"Is everything all right?" asked a thin, delicate voice.

Mr. Tidwell!

"I have to get home," Susan stammered, backing away from the dollhouse. "Come on, Kelly."

Grabbing Kelly's arm, Susan started to run to the door. But her shoulder hit a pyramid of stacked boxes, and she, Kelly, and the boxes fell to the floor.

"Do be careful, my dears," Mr. Tidwell said. "You'll hurt yourselves."

He stretched out a hand to Susan.

It was pale and wrinkled. Just like the hand in her dream.

She scrambled to her feet and pulled Kelly up, then hastily restacked the boxes.

"Sorry," she said over her shoulder to Mr. Tidwell. Then the two girls ran out the door, through the corridors of the mall, and out the Hill Street entrance.

"I wish we'd brought our bikes," Kelly panted. "I'm not into this jogging stuff."

"Just a couple more blocks," urged Susan.

Kelly was coming up the driveway, breathing hard, when Susan was fumbling with her key in the lock. Throwing open the door, she ran into the foyer.

"Mom!" she yelled.

And then she saw her.

Mrs. Martin was lying at the bottom of the stairs—just as the mother doll had been in the dollhouse.

"Mom!" Susan cried again, dropping to her knees beside her mother. "Are you all right?"

Mrs. Martin opened her eyes and tried to smile. "Would you believe I stepped on Howie's little red fire truck and did a really spectacular skid down that last flight of stairs?"

She closed her eyes and groaned. "Oh, Susan. I'm so glad you're here. I think I've broken my leg."

Fourteen

Both the ambulance and Mr. Martin arrived at the same time. Mr. Martin went off to the hospital with his wife, leaving Susan and Kelly to stay with Howie.

Howie was screaming in his playpen, so Susan changed his diaper, which calmed him down. Then she brought him into the kitchen and put apple juice in his little lidded mug. He liked that mug. It had pictures of a little bear named Tommy Tweedle on it.

Soon he was in a good humor again, but his eyelids were drooping.

"Nappy time, Howie," Susan said, lifting him out of his high chair.

Kelly watched with great interest.

"I wish I had a baby brother," she said. "You sure do miss out on a lot, being an only child."

Then the girls put Howie down for a nap and went into Susan's room.

"So this is what the turret room looks like from the inside," Kelly said. She looked around. "You're right, Susan. Mr. Tidwell's arranged the dollhouse turret room exactly like yours."

Her tone was light, but her eyes were worried.

Susan hadn't cried when she'd found her mother on the floor. Or when the paramedics had taken her off to the emergency room. But now, with her friend looking at her like that, so sympathetic and caring, everything hit her.

The way her mother had looked lying there, in pain but trying to make a little joke of her fall so she wouldn't worry Susan.

The evil that seemed to surround the dollhouse. The evil she didn't know how to fight.

Was there no way out? No way to escape this nightmare?

Suddenly she started to cry. "What's happening to all of us?" she sobbed. "And what will happen next?"

She buried her face in her hands.

"Susan!" Kelly's face was pale. She held out a trembling, pointing hand. For a moment she reminded Susan of one of the witches in last year's Halloween pageant—the one who was supposed to be laying a curse on the frog prince.

Kelly's mouth worked a couple of times before she could get the words out. "Susan . . . the way you're sitting on the bed . . . the way you're holding your head. *That's exactly what the sister doll was doing in the dollhouse!*"

"Okay," said Kelly when Susan had blown her nose and washed her face. "Now that you've got that out of your system, what are we gonna do about the dollhouse?"

The way she said "we" made Susan feel much, much better.

"I don't know, Kelly. I've got to think about it."

"Well, so will I," Kelly said. "Between the two of us, we're bound to come up with something."

By the time Kelly left, Susan was beginning to feel as if she might have a chance against the dollhouse. A chance to win.

Fifteen

It didn't take long for Mrs. Martin to learn how to get around on her crutches. In fact, in a couple of days, she was ready to run races on them. Or at least that's what she said.

She could even go up and down the stairs.

Going up was the hardest. But she came down on her bottom. "Maybe I'll bump off a couple of inches this way," she said hopefully.

Susan didn't want to say anything about the dollhouse and all the terrible things that had happened in connection with it. Her parents had enough on their minds. Besides, they would probably think she was having mental problems if she tried to explain what was going on.

And then they'd probably send her to a child psychiatrist at a jillion dollars an hour, and they couldn't afford that.

Why was all this happening to them? That's what she couldn't figure out. What had they done?

She and Kelly talked about it a lot.

There was obviously a connection between the dollhouse and the house. That was for sure. But what? And why?

And what about Mr. Tidwell? Did he have anything to do with all the strange things that were happening, or was he just the shopkeeper?

Susan and Kelly even called the Better Business Bureau about him. Kelly put a handkerchief over the telephone mouthpiece and disguised her voice in an attempt to sound older, while Susan listened in on another line. But they didn't have anything on him. In fact, they didn't even have a record of any Once and Forever Toy Shop at the Hingham Hill Mall. Or anywhere.

"Are you sure it's in the mall?" asked the woman at the Better Business Bureau, who identified herself only as Gladys.

"Yes, I thought maybe you could tell me how long the shop's been in business there," Kelly said, trying not to speak in her usual high-pitched voice. "I—uh—heard they're having some problems."

"Well, we have no record of such a place," Gladys said briskly.

She sounded bored. Susan could have sworn she was chewing bubble gum, too.

"I don't know how the private eyes do it," Kelly told Susan after they had hung up. "Maybe I just don't have the knack."

Susan felt as if a cloud was hanging over her.

At school, she laughed and joked with all the kids. They seemed to like her. She'd even been elected Corresponding Secretary for her class, not that they corresponded with anyone.

She and Mark had progressed to the smiling-at-each-other stage. Kelly told her there was a rumor going around that Mark had put a lot of pressure on his friends to vote for her for Corresponding Secretary. He was class Vice President and there would be staff meetings after school. And who knew what exciting, romantic things would come of that?

And yet . . .

And yet her mind turned back to the dollhouse all the time. Searching it. Trying to discover its secret.

She would lie in bed, picturing it in that archway at The Once and Forever Toy Shop, after the mall was locked up and all the lights were out.

She saw the dollhouse crouching in the shadows like an avenging gnome.

She saw the tiny windows lit up with an eerie, green glow. The glow of an evil force.

And so, even with all the good things that were happening to her at school, fear and worry burned in her stomach like acid.

It was hard for her to eat, or do her homework.

And it was very, very hard for her to sleep at night.

Sixteen

Susan wondered why the house was so quiet when she came home from school. It had been a dark, rainy day, yet no lights were on.

"Mom!" she yelled, coming into the foyer and throwing her schoolbooks down on the table. "I'm home!"

Suddenly the lights all came on.

"Happy un-birthday!" shouted her mother and father.

"Piz-za!" shouted Howie.

"Dad!" Susan exclaimed. "What are you doing home?"

Her parents and Howie were in the living room. Something big and wrapped in colorful paper was on the floor.

Susan walked slowly into the living room. "What's going on?"

Mrs. Martin leaned forward on her crutches, sticking out her broken leg with its cast and pale, bare toes. She looked pleased with herself.

"Your birthday isn't for another month, so we're celebrating it ahead of time, darling."

"But why?" asked Susan.

"Because you've been such a good kid about this move, that's why."

Her mother hobbled over and gave her a big hug and kiss.

"It was all your mother's idea," her father said modestly.

"Yes," Mrs. Martin admitted with a big smile. "It was." She took Susan's arm and led her over to the package. Putting her crutches together, she sank down on a sofa.

"You've been wanting something for a long time," she said. "And so your father and I decided we'd get it for you. Now. Not later, but now. This move has been hard on you, but you've been really good about it, and we're proud of you. Besides," she added, "we were afraid Mr. Tidwell would sell it before your birthday rolled around and it was just too big to try and hide until your birthday."

Mr. Tidwell?

Susan's heart sank. She knew what that big, brightly wrapped present was now.

A cold shiver ran down her spine, and the hairs on her arms stood on end.

It was here. In their house. The evil dollhouse.

Right here, in this room with her mom, her dad, and little Howie. And she'd *asked* for it. No— *begged* for it.

"Open it up!" her father said. "I've taken a half day off from work for this. Your poor mother couldn't bring it home on her crutches."

Howie was clearly into the spirit of the celebration. He joyously shouted out his entire vocabulary. "Ma-ma! Da-da! Piz-za!"

"Oh, this is so exciting." Susan hoped her voice sounded as thrilled as they expected it to be. "What on *earth* could it be?"

She knelt before the package. Carefully she grasped the edge of the paper and pulled. The paper ripped in half, and there, just as she'd dreaded, was the dollhouse turret.

At that instant, everything turned black. The lights flickered. The room was momentarily cast in shadow.

Mrs. Martin looked around. "Henry, are we having a power failure?"

But then the lights all came back on.

"The dollhouse!" Susan cried, trying to look

surprised and thrilled. "I can't believe it!"

She thought about the cost. And about how difficult it must have been for her parents to go to the mall to buy it— Mom on her crutches and Dad carrying fat, wriggly little Howie.

Then Dad taking an afternoon off to go pick it up. And then wrapping it and waiting so happily for her to come home from school. . . .

She felt a prickling in her eyes and throat when she said, "Oh, Mom! Dad! I love it." She wondered if she would be struck down for lying.

"Wait, there's more." Mrs. Martin fished around under the skirt of the sofa and came up with another large box.

"There's furniture, too," she said. "We haven't seen it yet, but it comes with the house. Mr. Tidwell had it all boxed up. Isn't that funny? He said he had a feeling he'd be selling the dollhouse, and wanted to be ready when it happened."

I'll bet he did, Susan thought miserably. *And I bet he knew who would be coming in to buy it, too!*

"You mean, you got me the furniture, too? Oh, I don't know what to say!" she cried.

And what will they say when they see that it's our furniture? And that the dolls are us? No! I've got to keep that from them. . . .

Susan kissed her mother, then went over to her father and kissed him, too.

"Thanks, Mom. Thank you, Dad. This is the happiest un-birthday I've ever had. And the nicest present," she lied.

Her parents beamed at each other.

"Aren't you going to let us see the furniture?" her father asked.

"Uh—no, not yet," she said quickly. "I mean, I'd like to arrange it in the house first, and then you can see it."

"What a nice idea," Mrs. Martin said. "Was it a surprise, darling? We hoped it would be."

"Believe me," Susan said honestly, "that dollhouse was the last thing I ever expected to see in this house."

"And now you have an errand to run, don't you, Henry?" Susan's mother said. "Involving cake and ice cream."

She turned to Susan and said, "It might not be your real birthday, but we're going all the way. To heck with the calories, full speed ahead."

When Susan was alone in her room she sat on the edge of the bed and put her head in her hands.

What can I do? she wondered desperately. *What*

can I do to protect my family? Mom. Dad. Little Howie.

She had a terrible feeling that the evil of the dollhouse was growing. And that it would destroy the people she loved most.

Seventeen

Susan helped her father carry the dollhouse up to her room that night after supper. It was lighter than it looked, but it was bulky. It took both of them to get it around the turn in the stairs.

They set it up on a card table in front of the turret window. Mrs. Martin had contributed an old fringed velvet cloth to put underneath it. The dollhouse sat there looking elegant and perfect—just as it had in the shop, when Susan had looked at it and wanted it more than anything in the world.

And now she wished it were gone. Gone from her house and gone from her life.

It was a good thing the next day was Saturday, because Susan was awake half the night wondering what she should do.

She would have to put the furniture and dolls in the dollhouse, she decided. Otherwise, her parents would ask questions. Besides, if something terrible was going to happen to her and her family, she'd like to get a little advance warning by seeing it happen in the dollhouse first.

But what would her parents say when they saw that the furniture matched the furniture in the house? And that the dolls looked like them?

They didn't know about the hidden latch that popped up the back wall of the dollhouse. She would pretend she didn't know where it was, either, and that she would have to check with Mr. Tidwell. Then the only way they could see inside the dollhouse would be through the windows, and if she kept the curtains on them half drawn . . .

But how would they think she got the furniture into the house? Would they believe her if she said she'd had to push it in through the doors?

Susan knew the time was coming when she had to tell her parents everything, and yet she knew they wouldn't believe it anyway. Who would? Who would believe there was such a thing as an evil, haunted dollhouse?

Kelly came over right after breakfast.

"Do you want to ride bikes?" she asked.

"Okay," said Susan. "But there's something upstairs I want you to see first."

Kelly came into the turret bedroom. When she

saw the dollhouse, she took a step backward, bumping into Susan. She stared silently at it for a long time. Then she turned to Susan, a look of horror on her face.

"What—what's *that* doing here?" she stammered.

Susan pushed her into the room and shut the door behind them. "My parents got it for me as sort of an advance birthday present. You've got to help me figure out what to do."

"This is awful," Kelly said. Her voice rose. "Something terrible is going to happen now. I just know it!" Suddenly she looked embarrassed. "I'm sorry, Susan. I just—"

"Listen, Kelly. I'm going to go see Mr. Tidwell again. He's got to tell me what's going on."

Kelly moaned softly. "Not again. It's like going into the Twilight Zone. And do you really think he'll tell you anything?"

"Maybe," Susan said. "I didn't get the chance to ask him the last time, remember? We ran out pretty fast when we saw what happened to the mother doll."

She went over to the closet and pulled out a light jacket. "You don't have to come with me. It's better if you don't get mixed up in it."

"Do you really think I'd let you go there alone?"

Kelly demanded. "Who knows what that creepy old man is planning to do. Maybe he plans to kidnap you. I sure don't want you to be the next face on a milk carton. It would turn a lot of little kids off milk."

It didn't take them long to bicycle to the mall.

"This sure beats jogging," Kelly called back over her shoulder.

The mall was nearly empty when they got there. Stores were just opening up. A few early-bird shoppers were looking in windows, but the mall hadn't started to fill up yet.

The corridor where The Once and Forever Toy Shop stood was deserted. Most of the little boutiques hadn't opened yet.

The curtain was drawn on the toy shop door. "It's not open," said Susan.

"Maybe," Kelly said, trying the door handle. It was unlocked, and the girls pushed the door open and entered the shop.

It was empty. All the toys were gone. And the shelves and counters, too. There was nothing there but an empty room. And beyond that another empty room.

"He's gone!" Susan said, stepping into the middle of the room.

"Not yet, my dear," said a voice behind her.

Susan whipped around. Mr. Tidwell was standing there, smiling.

This time, Susan knew he hadn't been behind a counter or in another room. There was no place he could have been hiding.

He was simply not there one second and there the next.

"Are you pleased with your parents' little present?" he asked. "In case you are worried about the price, I gave them a very fine deal." He coughed delicately. "I could afford to. I expect to . . . er . . . receive many benefits from this transaction."

Kelly and Susan exchanged a long look. Then Kelly punched Susan in the side, as a signal Susan should do the talking.

Susan cleared her throat. "That's what we've come to find out, Mr. Tidwell. What *do* you think you're going to get out of this deal?"

"Yeah, what?" chimed in Kelly.

"What I usually get," said Mr. Tidwell. He pulled out an antique pocket watch and consulted it, as if he had an appointment somewhere else soon.

"You see, I'm what you might call a broker," he went on. "A broker in wishes, to be more precise."

Susan swallowed. "I don't know what you're talking about," she whispered hoarsely.

"It's really very simple," Mr. Tidwell went on, sounding slightly impatient. "I give people what they think they want, and then I get the pleasure of seeing their wishes come true." He shook his head and laughed. "And that house on Pine Street is so beautiful. I just knew someone like you would want it for her very own . . ."

"Are you crazy or am I?" Kelly blurted out. She turned to Susan. "What does he mean?"

Susan didn't reply. She had to find out a few more things first. "Who built that dollhouse, Mr. Tidwell?"

"Why—who do you think, Susan?" he replied. "I did, of course." His ice-blue eyes bored into hers. "Yes, I'm very good with my hands. I find certain things so easy to . . . ah . . . manipulate. I'm quite inventive, in case you haven't noticed."

He made a quick gesture, and a black umbrella appeared in his hand.

"But—but I don't understand. . ." Susan whispered.

Mr. Tidwell sighed. "I'll try to make a long story short, as I have miles to go before I sleep. When your eyes fell upon that dollhouse, you wanted it, no? You wished more than anything in the whole world that you could live inside it, that you could walk through its rooms, that you could sleep in

101

that little tower. And your wishes came true!"

Susan opened her mouth, but no words came out. She was too horrified to speak.

Mr. Tidwell shook his head and made a faint tut-tutting sound. "But that wasn't quite good enough, was it? Then you wished to own the dollhouse as well. And now you do. You see, my dear, wishes are forever. Of course, most people don't realize the consequences. . . ."

"The consequences?" Kelly asked.

"Oh, yes. You see, your friend here wished to live in the dollhouse forever and ever. And now she will. Because, you see, that house on Pine Street *is* the dollhouse." He smiled, sending terrible shivers up Susan's spine. "They're one and the same. There's no escape."

"But why?" Susan finally managed. "Why *me*?"

Mr. Tidwell laughed out loud. "Indeed, why not? I do the same for *all* my customers."

Susan shook her head. "All your customers?" she repeated.

"Oh, yes." Mr. Tidwell nodded, looking pleased with himself. "Of course, I have to tailor my sales pitch to suit each customer. Some want toys. Some want games. But when I saw you, I knew you were a natural for the dollhouse." He chuckled. "The dolls were just a little something extra. Without the dollhouse, they're nothing but bits of wire and clay."

Kelly pulled at Susan's jacket.

"Susan," she said in a terrified whisper. "I think we better get out of here."

Mr. Tidwell held up a pale, wrinkled hand. "Yes, it's time we part." He flashed another quick smile. "Good-bye, my dears. Perhaps we'll meet again."

And with that, he was gone.

Eighteen

Susan and Kelly found themselves sitting on a bench in the Clock Court. They had no idea how they'd gotten there.

Kelly moaned, held out her arm, and pushed back her sleeve. "Quick, Susan. Pinch me hard. I'm having a terrible nightmare and I want to wake up."

"It's not a nightmare," Susan told her. "It's really happening."

Kelly looked dazed. "What are we doing here? And what time is it?" She turned around to look at the big clock with the castle on its top. "It's already ten o'clock."

Susan shook her head. "No. You know what time it is, Kelly? It's time to get rid of that doll-house—for good."

"How?" asked Kelly.

104

"I'm going to burn it," Susan said grimly. "Destroy it completely, before it does any more harm. And then I'm going to tell my folks everything. I'll make them believe me. We have to move out of that house."

Kelly nodded. "I'm coming with you."

Mrs. Martin struggled to her feet when the girls came into the house.

"You've come just in the nick of time," she told them. "I have errands to run, and I can only do them when Dad can drive me. This broken leg has really grounded me."

Susan and Kelly exchanged glances. Both Susan's mom and her dad would be out. Perfect. This would make it easier to burn the dollhouse. Susan had been wondering how they'd manage it.

"We'll probably be a couple of hours," Mrs. Martin went on, "so I'll pay you both for baby-sitting Howie. It's only fair, since it's Saturday and you have things to do."

Do we ever! thought Susan.

"Dad's put Howie's playpen in the little TV room, so he's happy watching cartoons. He usually falls asleep watching them. I've put his blanket and teddy in there with him."

"Okay, Mom," Susan said, trying to sound as cheerful as possible. "No problem."

The minute Mr. and Mrs. Martin drove off, Susan and Kelly bolted upstairs to Susan's bedroom.

Susan shuddered a little when she looked at the dollhouse. Well, it would soon be gone. And then, with luck, she could talk her parents into moving out of the house.

Scooping the little dolls from the house, Susan said, "This thing isn't as heavy as it looks. But it's hard to get around corners because it's so big."

"I sure hope I'm not the one who has to go down the stairs backward," said Kelly.

Susan thought for a minute. "Maybe we can put it on a rug and just kind of pull it along and down the stairs."

"Now you're talking."

The dollhouse started going down the stairs pretty fast and made a lot of noise as it thumped down the last flight. Susan had to go into the little TV room off the living room to make sure it hadn't frightened Howie. He was sound asleep on the floor of his playpen, his blanket held to his cheek and his thumb in his mouth.

So far so good.

"We're going to have to go out the front door,"

Susan said, "and over to that empty lot across the street. There's a big area behind the new house that's being built where they burn trash. I've seen them do it."

"Won't they be surprised Monday morning when they find burned parts of a dollhouse out there?" Kelly said.

"No. There's some lighter fluid in the garage that Dad uses for the charcoal grill. If I use enough, the dollhouse ought to burn right up. It's old and the wood must be dried out."

"Wait," Kelly said as they got to the front door. "What if somebody sees us carrying this? They might try to stop us."

"Good thinking," Susan said. She ran upstairs and came down with a sheet. "This is an old one. It won't matter if it goes."

She threw the sheet over the dollhouse, covering it completely. "There," she said.

It seemed to get dark in the house suddenly. "Oh-oh," said Kelly. "I hope it's not going to rain on our bonfire."

Susan opened the front door. The sun was shining. "Hmm," she said, feeling a strange tingling feeling at the back of her neck. "A cloud must have just passed in front of the sun."

They looked both ways as they walked across the

front yard. The street was deserted. Good. They carried the dollhouse across the street and behind the half-built house. It wasn't bad carrying the house out in the open, where they didn't have to worry about bumping things or going around corners or down stairs.

They set the house down in the blackened ashes of previous fires. Susan threw a handful of dried grass into the air. It fell straight down.

"Good," she said. "There's no wind today. We don't have to worry about the fire getting away from us."

"Okay, here goes," she said, pulling the cap off the lighter fluid. It was a large container and she used it all, pouring it over the roof and porch and down the sides of the little house.

"Stand back," she said at last, setting the empty fluid can down at a safe distance and striking a match. "Are you ready?"

Kelly nodded. She looked pale, and her eyes were twice their usual size.

The house went up immediately. In less than a minute, the entire house was burning. Everything, that is, except the small room by the living room that jutted out from the first floor.

Susan frowned. She shouldn't have used all the lighter fluid. She could have given that area an extra squirt, but at the rate the fire was spreading, it would be burning soon.

A feeling of relief came over Susan. She had done the right thing. She was sure of that now. Her family was out of danger.

She could just stand here and watch it burn. . . .

"No," she heard Kelly whisper. "Susan, look!"

Susan turned around. Across the street, a plume of black smoke was rising from . . . *Oh, no!*

Her *real* house was on fire.

Her mind whirled. Howie . . . Howie was in the house. . . .

She and Kelly tore across the lot and into her yard. Several of her neighbors were standing on the sidewalk, talking excitedly. She could hear the faraway wailing of fire trucks.

Susan knew right away they wouldn't come in time to save Howie.

It was up to her to save him.

Nineteen

How could she have been so stupid?

She should have known that whatever happened to the dollhouse would happen to the real one, too. Mr. Tidwell's words rang in her head: *"That house on Pine Street* is *the dollhouse."*

Some of the neighbors tried to grab her and stop her as she raced up the walk.

"My brother's in there!" Susan shouted, wrenching free of the clutching hands.

The front porch was in flames, so Susan ran around the side of the house. There was a window to the TV room. Sometimes they kept it open. She prayed it would be open today.

It was! But how could she possibly reach it? It was set up too high in the wall.

She heard rapid footsteps, coming around the corner behind her.

110

Kelly!

Kelly ran up to her, knelt on the ground, and bent over. "Here, Susan. Stand on my back."

Susan crawled up on Kelly's back and tore at the screen. It was old and rusty, and pulled away easily. Then, throwing a leg over the windowsill, she scrambled into the room.

Howie was awake and shrieking like a stuck pig. Susan heaved a huge sigh of relief. It was the most beautiful sound she had ever heard in her life.

She could see the flames running, like busy little fingers, up the sides of the open doorway that led into the TV room. It wouldn't be long now before the entire room was on fire.

Grabbing Howie up from his playpen, she crossed to the window in a few giant steps. She could feel the heat on her back. Howie was flinging his arms around wildly in his terror. One chubby fist caught her square in the eye, but she blinked back the tears and kept on going.

By now, a group of people had gathered beneath the window. When she held Howie out, anxious hands were stretched up to take him.

The netting on the sides of the playpen had already begun to burn when she threw a leg over the windowsill and dropped to the ground.

Something broke her fall when she hit.

Something soft. Something that said, "Ooof. Jeez, Susan, why don't you lose some weight!"

Kelly!

Susan rolled off her onto the ground, laughing and crying all at once. Howie was busy deafening everyone present with his earsplitting screams.

The last of the house burst into flames.

And then the firemen arrived.

Twenty

Nothing was left of the big old house on Pine Street. Nothing but a wet pile of smoldering, blackened rubble.

So Mr. Tidwell was wrong, after all, Susan told herself. *Not all wishes are forever.*

The thought cheered her up, in spite of the fact that she, her parents, and Howie were sitting on a wet curb, with nothing but the clothes on their backs. And those clothes weren't in very good shape, either.

Susan had been hailed as the heroine of the year. TV crews had come and gone. There was even talk of her meeting the mayor at a special awards banquet.

Her mother and father had told her over and over again what a wonderful, brave girl she was to risk her life like that to save Howie, and every neighbor on their block had invited them to be their guests while they looked for a new house.

Kelly had finally gone home. But Susan knew they'd be seeing a lot of each other in the future. Kelly's parents had said that Susan could stay at their house for a while.

"Well," Mr. Martin said slowly, "I guess we'll have to start over. Thank heaven we were heavily insured."

"Look at it this way, Henry," said Mrs. Martin. "We won't have to do all that heavy fall cleaning we've been dreading." A hysterical laugh escaped her lips—a laugh that quickly turned into wild crying, and before she was done the whole family, including Howie, had joined in.

"Oh my," she said at last, blowing her nose on a ratty tissue she'd dredged up from a pocket. "I needed that."

"We could rebuild on this lot," suggested Mr. Martin, wiping his eyes on a grimy sleeve.

"Forget it," said Mrs. Martin. "Let's buy a nice, modern little house somewhere else. This place has been jinxed from the start. All that stuff the moving men replaced with wood." She paused. "And, to tell you the truth," she added quietly, "I was starting to feel there was something . . . well . . . not quite right about that house."

"The fire chief said the ancient wiring in this house must have caused the fire," Mr. Martin said thoughtfully. "He couldn't think of any other way it could have spread so quickly through the entire house."

Right, Susan thought. *It's not like a giant stood there and sprayed lighter fluid all over it or anything.*

"The important thing," Mrs. Martin said, gathering her children closer to her, "the *most* important thing is that the kids are okay, and that we're all together."

Susan smiled. "You got that right."

Epilogue

It was months before Susan could muster the courage to go back to the mall.

After her family moved into their new house, she did her best not to think of the whole terrible ordeal. Luckily, there was nothing about the new house that could remind her of the old place on Pine Street. Her parents had found a cozy little redbrick home in a nearby neighborhood—two stories tall with black shutters and a big chimney.

There was nothing spooky about it at all.

Every now and then, Kelly would suggest going to the mall after school. Susan always found an excuse not to go, even though Kelly promised her that Mr. Tidwell was gone and that there was another toy store in the spot where The Once and Forever Toy Shop had been.

Susan didn't want to go anywhere near the place.

But finally, on a bright spring day, she decided she was being silly. She couldn't stay away from the mall for the rest of her life. Besides, Mr. Tidwell had been wrong. She had escaped the house on Pine Street. Wishes *weren't* forever.

Susan met Kelly at her house and the two rode their bikes over to the mall.

"You should really check out the new toy store," Kelly said as they walked through the big glass doors and headed toward the Clock Court. "It's nothing like Mr. Tidwell's shop. It's got all kinds of cool electronic games and stuff."

"Sure," Susan said.

And then she felt it. That old shivery feeling she used to get . . .

They turned into the corridor where Mr. Tidwell's Once and Forever Toy Shop had been.

Susan stared at the new store. Kelly was right—it *did* look cool. For one thing, it wasn't run-down like Mr. Tidwell's shop had been. It had a huge glass window behind which were hanging model airplanes, toy cars, stuffed animals . . .

Susan's eyes fell to the farthest corner of the window.

And then her heart jumped in her chest.

Because there, sitting on a red velvet cloth, was a dollhouse. A two-story, redbrick dollhouse, with black shutters and a big chimney.

It was Susan's house.

Her *new* house.

She screamed.

About the Author

Bebe Faas Rice was born in Philadelphia but grew up in Iowa and California. After graduating from college she joined the Marine Corps and was sent to Washington, D.C., where she met her husband. As a Marine Corps wife she has lived in twenty-four different homes on posts and stations both in this country and overseas. She and her husband have one son.

Ms. Rice is the author of numerous young adult and juvenile novels, including the Edgar-nominated novel *Class Trip*.